Circus Fun!

Elizabeth Dale

Illustrated by
Vicki Gausden

EGMONT

We bring stories to life

Book Band: Orange

First published in Great Britain 2014
by Egmont UK Ltd
The Yellow Building, 1 Nicholas Road, London W11 4AN
Text copyright © Elizabeth Dale 2014
Illustrations copyright © Vicki Gausden 2014
The author and illustrator have asserted their moral rights.
ISBN 978 1 4052 7069 4
www.egmont.co.uk
10 9 8 7 6 5 4 3 2 1
A CIP catalogue record for this title is available from the British Library.
Printed in Singapore.
57029/1

EGMONT LUCKY COIN

Our story began over a century ago, when seventeen-year-old Egmont Harald Petersen found a coin in the street.

He was on his way to buy a flyswatter, a small hand-operated printing machine that he then set up in his tiny apartment.

The coin brought him such good luck that today Egmont has offices in over 30 countries around the world. And that lucky coin is still kept at the company's head offices in Denmark.

Coco Joins the Circus

Coco the Tightrope Walker

Coco the Clown

For my grandson, Leo,
who's always a bundle of fun!
E. D.

For Egg

V. G.

Coco
Joins the Circus

TICKETS

Coco was thrilled when he saw the tents. He had always wanted to be in the circus.

Can I join?

'We need someone to ride a unicycle,'

said the Ringmaster. 'Can you do that?'

'Of course!' said Coco.

Coco was so excited. He didn't know what a unicycle was. But he wasn't going to say that!

Maybe it was a unicorn on wheels?

'Here you go!' said the Ringmaster.

Coco gasped. The bike had only

one wheel!

How could he balance on that?!

Coco sat on the bike.

He put his feet on the pedals
and wibbled . . . and wobbled.

Suddenly someone gave him a push.
Coco pedalled really fast. He was
cycling! Yippee! This was fun!

Coco followed the others into
the ring. The crowd clapped.

Just do what
Maria does!

Coco stuck out one leg, just like Maria.

Then Maria put one foot on her saddle. Coco did, too . . .

Then Maria stood up.

Coco was scared, but he stood up, too.

He wibbled . . .

. . . and wobbled . . .

. . . and fell off.

Uh . . . oh!

The crowd laughed.

They thought he meant to fall.

Everyone clapped, so Coco bowed and smiled.

Why are they all clapping?

Coco
the Tightrope Walker

Coco knew he was useless at the unicycle. But he loved the circus. 'Can I stay?' he begged.

Okay . . . I have the perfect job for you!

Coco didn't like his new job very much. He really wanted to make people smile.

So he sang as he worked.

Crowds flocked to hear him and buy his candy floss.

Coco just couldn't keep up!

So he made his machine go faster.

The Ringmaster asked Coco to walk

along the rope on the grass.

It was easy!

'Well done!' said the Ringmaster.

'You can walk the tightrope.'

Coco was so excited. He had a shiny

costume to wear.

He practised and practised.

Perfect!

At last it was time to go on!

The tightrope was so high.

Somehow walking up there felt

very different.

Coco wibbled . . .

Uh . . .
Oh!

and wobbled . .

And then he fell.

Right on to the Ringmaster!

Sorry!

The crowd laughed and laughed.

Suddenly Coco saw Maria swinging

very high. What if she fell?!

Coco ran to and fro, ready to catch her.

But he was too busy looking up . . .

Ugh!

. . . to see where he was going!

Sorry!

Coco knew he'd really done it this time.

He would have to go.

Waa aah!

Coco began to leave the ring. But the Ringmaster caught hold of Coco's arm as the crowd laughed and cheered.

'You can't go,' he told Coco.

'You're a star!'

Coco
the Clown

When the Ringmaster asked Coco to be a clown, just for that night, Coco jumped for joy.

'I've always wanted to be a clown!'

he cried. 'But I didn't think I was

funny enough.'

You are very funny – when you're not trying to be!

STARRING

Coco the

CLOWN!

They looked for a costume for Coco.

But nothing fitted.

Wear these to keep your trousers up.

The crowd cheered as Coco ran in.

But suddenly – **SNAP!**

Coco's trousers fell down.

As Coco bent to pick them up,

his hat fell off.

Archie stood in it by mistake.

Coco chased him.

Archie drove away in his car – fast.

Coco jumped on the back . . .

. . . and fell off!

Everyone laughed. Coco grinned.

This was fun!

Suddenly he saw the custard pies.

Coco meant to miss Archie.

But he didn't!

As Archie chased him, Coco tripped

over his big boots . . .

. . . and Archie tripped over Coco.

Quickly, Coco squirted Archie with water from his big plastic flower.

But he got the crowd instead!

The crowd laughed and laughed.

Archie and Coco bowed . . .

. . . bumped bottoms . . .

. . . and fell over again!

The crowd cheered.

'Coco!' cried the Ringmaster.

'You're so funny! Will you be our clown

for good?'

Coco couldn't speak.

But his big smile gave everyone

his answer.

He was a clown at last!